Crackers

"Right," said Sandy. "I claim these premises for Crackers. May God bless her and all who sail in her."

"Hang on a minute," I said. "That's for a ship, isn't it? And keep your voice down. You don't want the whole school to know."

"Stop arguing," said Sandy, "and listen to your instructions. Our next meeting is tomorrow, in these premises, at first break, and you'll have to bring two more pages, because we're going to bring out the first issue two weeks from today."

Also by Elizabeth Laird

On the Run

for older readers

Hiding Out
(Winner of the Smarties Award)
Jay
(Winner of the Lancashire Book Award)
Kiss the Dust
(Winner of the Children's Book Award)

Elizabeth Laird
CRACKERS

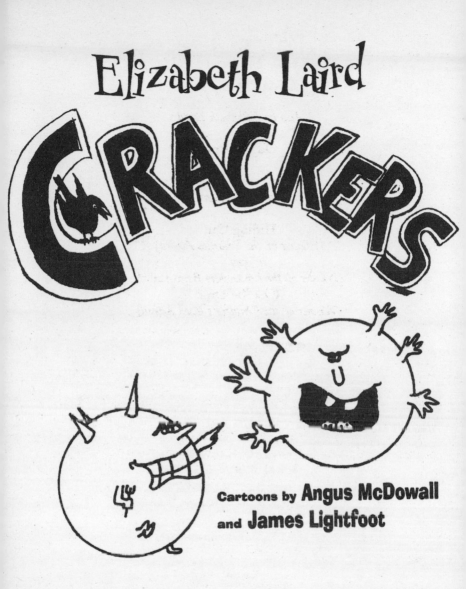

**Cartoons by Angus McDowall
and James Lightfoot**

Mammoth

This book is dedicated to
JAMES D., JAMES L., SAM, JIM,
EDWARD and ANGUS

First published in Great Britain 1989
by Heinemann Young Books
Published 1990 by Mammoth
Reissued 1998 by Mammoth
an imprint of Egmont Children's Books Limited
239 Kensington High Street, London W8 6SA

ISBN 0 7497 0309 1

10 9 8 7 6 5 4

A CIP catalogue record for this title
is available from the British Library

Printed in Great Britain
by Cox & Wyman Ltd, Reading, Berkshire

Chapter One

You know the Champ? It's the greatest. It's number one, top of the charts, world class. It's my favourite comic. It's got the Gobbledegooks, and Swizzle the Seal, and Loopy Len. It's miles and miles better than all the others, like the Fizz, that only softies read, and Tiddles, that's really babyish.

You can't say that to my Mum though. She doesn't like the Champ. She can't stand me reading comics all the time. There I am, sitting comfortably on the sofa in our living room, and she comes along and says, "Why don't you read a proper book for a change?"

And then she sort of sighs, and says, "You'll never get on at school if you only read that kind of rubbish."

So I pretend I haven't heard, and her voice goes up a bit higher, and she says, "Polly read *The Jungle Book* when she was only eight." (Polly's my sister and she's a real teacher's pet.)

"What about Dave then?" I always say. "He never even reads the back of the Cornflakes packet."

Dave's my big brother, and he had advanced brain death when he was my age. He's brilliant now though. It just goes to show.

What Mum doesn't know is that I do read books, sometimes. I've read *The Jungle Book* anyway. But I sort of do it when she's not looking. I don't want her to start hoping I'll be a genius, like Polly. I'd never be able to keep it up.

So when I read a book I keep it private. I'm good at doing that, keeping secrets I mean, especially since we moved house and I got my own bedroom.

I'd be a fantastic spy, all cool and everything on top, and doing brilliant, dangerous things in the night that no one would ever have thought of. And then one day they'd make a film about me, and everyone would say, "Whew, Rick Sturgis, he's a dark horse. Who'd have thought it? Just seemed all ordinary, but really, underneath, wow!"

I don't think I'd like being a spy much though, because I wouldn't like murdering people all the time, and anyway, I want to be an artist. I'm going to do famous cartoons and get a job on the Champ.

I bet they'd like my frog character. My friend Sandy says it's brilliant. He came round to borrow some glue for his model aeroplane, and I was just pretending to be doodling while he hunted round on the table, and then I showed my picture to him, sort of casually, as if I'd just thought of it, when really I'd been practising for weeks, and he was dead impressed.

"You're a genius! Five star! Gold medal!" he

kept saying. That's just like Sandy. He's all or nothing. Always wild about something. He's not laid back, like me. Sandy couldn't keep a secret for five minutes. Or even two minutes. Or even ten seconds, come to think of it. I think it goes with having freckles.

Anyway, after he'd calmed down a bit, he said, "Why don't you call it Freddy Frog? That's a good name."

So I said, "No, that's silly."

And he said, "Well, Frankie then."

And I said, "Give me a break."

And he said, "What about Ferdinand."

And I said, "You must be joking."

Then he shut up for a bit.

"It doesn't have to start with 'f,'" I said.

"What about Hoppy?" he said.

"Too boring."

"Glossop then."

"What?"

"Glossop."

"Why Glossop?"

"Well, it sounds sort of squidgy, and wet, and croaky."

"Glossop," I said. "Glossop." I liked it. Give Sandy time, and he'll have a really great idea in the end.

Then he started being a twit, and jumping round my bedroom, pretending to look for a frog, shouting, "Glossie, Glossie! Come to Uncle Sandy!" only the idiot was still holding the glue. And Mum came in, and saw that the lid had

come off the tube, and the glue had got all over
the carpet. So that was the end of Sandy for that
day. Mum had him out of the house and me on
my hands and knees helping to scrub the carpet
in five minutes flat.

Chapter Two

Sandy and I go to school together most days. And every day except Tuesday, he's late. He sends me round the twist. We have to belt all the way up Park Hill Rise and down Penny Hill to get to school before the bell goes. It's all right for him. His mum wouldn't say much if she got a rude letter from Mr Crook (he's our Headmaster, and the name really suits him). But my dad would go for me.

It's different on Tuesday though. That's the day the Champ comes out. Sandy's on the doorstep while I'm still finishing my breakfast, and he's dragged me out of the house and up the road before I've had time to do up my shoelaces.

"Do them up!" shrieks Mum after me, so the whole street can hear, and I feel really awful in case everyone thinks she's talking about my trousers.

Mr Portman — he runs the corner shop — he's used to Sandy by now. Sandy doesn't even have to say anything. He just streaks through the door and slides to a halt at the counter. You know those little round sort of puffy clouds they do behind people's feet in comics when they're going really fast? Well, I've almost seen real ones behind Sandy on a Tuesday morning. Well, nearly, anyway.

Mr Portman's got these funny round specs because he's as blind as a bat, and he peers down his shop to see what's coming, and he fetches a Champ off the pile and hands it over, and Sandy whacks down the money, and then he goes all different. Sandy does, I mean. He gets his nose in his Champ, and wanders out of the shop, and he'd have to find his way to school by radar if I wasn't there.

Usually, I pull him along as if he was my pet dog or something. I say, "Halt," when we have to stop at the main road, and "Walkies," when we have to cross, and "Come on, doggie," when he slows down too much. He's so busy reading, he doesn't even notice. Not till we've got to school, anyway. Then I say, "Good dog, give it to me," and he wakes up, and realizes he's supposed to be a dog, and he tries to lick me, and I beat him off, and then we have a fight, and I get the Champ off him. I have ten minutes peace and quiet with it in the playground before the bell rings.

It's always Sandy who gets first read, though, because he's the one who buys it. He gets lots more pocket money than me. I suppose it's because he's an only child.

That's how it usually is, anyway. But one awful Tuesday, the Champ wasn't there. Old Sandy, same as usual, screeched up to the counter, plonked down his money, and waited. But Mr Portman shook his head.

"Distribution problems," he said. "They didn't send me more than a few this week. Strike or something, I suppose."

So instead of being a dog trainer, I had to be a life-support machine, all the way to school. You'd have thought it was the end of the world or something. Sandy's like that. He takes things big, Sandy does. Mum says it's because he gets his own way too often.

The next Tuesday, believe it or not, it happened again.

"Sorry, lads," said Mr Portman. "They've let me down again."

Well, I was disappointed, but I knew I'd get over it. Maybe I'm more used to disappointments than Sandy is or something. Anyway, he looked so miserable he could have been one of those corpses in scary cartoon films; you know, all pale, and ghostly and stiff.

And then all of a sudden his face went a sort of deep pink colour, and he's got this bright red hair so I practically needed my sunglasses. I thought he was going to burst, or have a heart attack or something, and he pointed over my shoulder, so I turned round, and what I saw nearly made me burst too.

Chapter Three

Right behind Mr Portman, jumping up and down, was Funny-Face Stevie, his horrible son, who goes around in Dudley Parker's gang. (Dudley Parker's the biggest bully this world has ever known.) And Stevie was sticking his disgusting slobbery tongue out, and waving a brand new Champ from behind his Dad's back, pointing at it in a really nasty, teasing way, and keeping well back in case Sandy did one of his famous roaring charges. You wouldn't believe what Sandy gets like when he's in a temper. I don't believe it myself, sometimes.

"Here, Mr Portman," I said, "Fun–, I mean, Stevie's got one. It's not fair."

"Only four in today," said Mr Portman, "and they all sold out soon as I undid them," and he dusted his precious packets of coffin nails. Bet you don't know what that means, so I'll tell you. Cigarettes.

"Yes," said Sandy, his voice all trembly, "but you've only just opened the shop, Mr Portman. No one else has come in yet. So who got the other three?"

Mr Portman didn't have a chance to answer because Stevie, still safely behind the counter, pulled out three more Champs from inside his smelly old jumper, and danced round pretending to be all babyish, and chanted, "One for Stevie, one for Dudley, one for Leroy, one for Pete," until Mr Portman suddenly got fed up, and turned round sharpish, and said, "Get out of here, you little pest," and swung his arm up to give him one, but Stevie nipped out before he could get him. I don't think Mr Portman would have hit him, anyway. For one thing he's too slow, and for another thing he's soft, Mr Portman is. He's really nice to kids, usually. I suppose that's why old Funny-Face is so spoilt.

"I'm going to get that Stevie Portman," said Sandy, when we got out into the street.

"Well," I said, trying to calm him down, as usual, "it is his dad that sells them . . ."

"It's not that," said Sandy. He did one of his fantastic kung fu kicks at Mr Portman's window, but stopped just in time so he didn't actually hit it. "Stevie shouldn't have teased me like that, waving it around, making me feel worse. I'm going to kick him black and blue and pull all his hair out."

"No, you're not," I said.

"I'm going to put ants in his trousers and mud in his lunchbox," said Sandy.

"No, you're not," I said, a bit louder.

"I'm going to chop up slugs and put them in his sandwiches," said Sandy.

"NO, YOU'RE NOT!" I shouted. He heard me at last.

"Why not?" he said.

"Because he's bigger than you," I said.

"What *am* I going to do then?" he said. I didn't have time to answer, because he was still doing his kung fu stunts, and by mistake he kicked an empty crisp packet and it whizzed up and landed in the bag of the postman who was going past. He's awful, our postman is. He's always cross about something, like when Mr McNulty's dog is out in the front garden, or when he gets scratched by the rose bush next door. I knew he'd go for us so we ran on fast, and he was too lazy to chase us.

Sandy's soggy crisp packet turned out to be lucky, because when we'd stopped running I had the best, the biggest, the most beautiful idea I'd ever had in my whole life.

"I know what we'll do," I said. "We'll make our own comic. We'll think up the characters, and do the stories, and draw it, and sell it at school. We'll make heaps and heaps of money. We'll be millionaires. We'll get so rich we'll be able to buy up all the Champs in the world, and we'll make Mr Smartypants Stevie and Mr Bullyboy Dudley pay a billion pounds just to borrow one for five minutes."

Chapter Four

Sandy's jaw had dropped open. If a whole family of flies had come along just then they could have flown straight into his mouth and down into his tum.

"I'll be the principal artist," I said, seeing the whole thing, perfect, in a sort of brilliant flash. "You can be the editor because you're good at spelling. There's lots of jobs they have to do, sort of organising everything. We'll put in Glossop the Frog, and I'll do the jokes, and . . ."

I'll say this for Sandy. He may have the hottest temper and the biggest mouth in the northern hemisphere, but he's quick. You don't usually have to say something sixty-five times to Sandy, and then write it down and draw a picture, like you do for poor old Dean. Sandy's sharp as razors.

"We'll get Zeb to do his Victor Vulture," he said.

I wasn't sure about that; bringing someone else in, I mean. After all, it was my idea, and I didn't fancy anyone else sort of coming along and taking it over. But Sandy was dead right. Zeb was great at drawing. After me, he's the best in our class, and one of the best in the school. Except for Bella, of course.

Bella's a girl, but I don't mind her really. She stuck up for me once when Stevie Portman said I'd deliberately trodden all over his model spaceship, and it had been that flat-footed idiot Mandy Cootes all the time. If Zeb was going to be in on this, I knew we'd have to ask Bella too.

"Let's get old Bella to do her Knutty Knitters," I said. "They're ace. All balls of wool everywhere, and everyone getting tangled up in them."

"Yeah, but she's a girl," said Sandy. He didn't need to say any more. I knew what he thought about girls.

"I know," I said, "but half the school's girls, and they've always got more money than the boys. They'd buy it for the Knitters."

"OK," said Sandy. "I suppose we could get her to do a special page for the girls or something."

But then I thought of something, and this time it was a real problem.

"How are we going to print it, then?" I said.

Sandy didn't answer. He'd disappeared. He's got this funny way of going down a road. He always bends over double and creeps along beside parked cars, then he straightens up again when he's past them. It takes him ages getting down Penny Hill when there's a lot of cars parked in it. It looks really funny. You see this red head going along all normal, then suddenly you blink and it's gone, and then up it pops again, like a flaming jack-in-the-box. Sandy says he does it because you never know who's in a parked car, and if there were gangsters in there with a machine gun, ready to rake the pavement with a hail of fire, he'd rather be out of the way, thank you very much.

"What makes you think there are gangsters in Penny Hill?" I say to him, but he just says, "What makes you think there aren't?"

It's just as well there's a stretch halfway down the road without any cars because after we'd got past the first few we managed to get on with making plans. I had another brainwave.

"Uncle Godfrey!" I said.

"Uncle what?" said Sandy.

"Godfrey."

"No-one's called Godfrey."

"Yes they are."

"Who is then?"

"My uncle, you idiot,"

"What about him, then?"

"He's got this sort of workshop," I explained, "out the back of his house, in a kind of big shed.

He runs a business. Sends out lots of envelopes, and works machines, and stuff."

"So what?" said Sandy. Did I say he was quick? Sometimes he could be thick as thick.

"He's got a photocopying machine," I said. "He lets me have a go on it sometimes. I bet he'd let us do our comic on it if I swept up the floor for him. It gets in an awful mess, and he's got a bad leg. And he's really nice to me, Uncle Godfrey is."

"Ricky, my son," said Sandy, pounding me on the back, right on top of the graze I'd got falling off the swings the day before, "you're the Brain of Bridgend School," and then he suddenly bobbed down again and started creeping along the pavement because we'd come up to Mrs Angelbeck's mini.

"Come off it," I said, "there aren't any gangsters in Mrs Angelbeck's mini."

"You've only got to get it wrong once," said Sandy. "I'm not taking any risks."

Chapter Five

The only trouble with brilliant ideas is that they stop you doing anything else. I couldn't think of another thing all morning.

"Class, get out your project books," said Miss Prout. At least, I think that's what she said. A long way off, I heard the usual sort of clatter, but as if it was on another planet. I was imagining a lovely, gleaming pile of new comics, and hundreds of eager kids with fistfuls of money queuing up to buy them, and all of them saying, "Have you seen this brilliant frog one? Must have been done by a professional. It's better than the Champ even."

Then all of a sudden, there was a silence, and I

looked up, and Miss Prout the Trout was standing right in front of me.

"You-have-been-hypnotized," she said in a sing-song voice. "Now-it-is-time-to-wake-up," and the rest of the class laughed. Mean lot, they are.

Breaktime seemed about a million years away, but it came at last. I was out in the playground a bit late, because I was asking Mandy where Bella was, and she said Bella was at the dentist, and I said it wasn't fair because my Mum always makes me go after school, and she said why did the dentist make me wear such a silly brace, and I said it wasn't silly, it was brilliant because it had a big plastic thing with wrinkles on it that matched the wrinkles in my mouth. I had to take it out to show her, and she stuck her filthy fingers all over it, so I had to go and wash it. And by the time I was outside, Sandy had vanished.

I spotted him at last behind a tree, talking to Zeb, so I launched a rocket attack and landed on them at the speed of light. It was a bit too sudden really because I knocked old Zeb off his feet, and Sandy lost his cool, and yelled, "Stop it you idiot, do you want everyone to see us?" which was even dafter, because half the playground might have heard and guessed we'd got a secret, if they hadn't all been so busy running away from Dudley Parker. I told you Sandy couldn't keep his mouth shut if you paid him.

We nearly had a flaming row after that, because usually Zeb's quite touchy about being pushed over, but I cunningly got their minds off it by saying, "What are we going to call it, then?"

And they both said, "Call what?"

And I said, "The comic."

And that got them so busy thinking they forgot about the fight.

"Let's make it sound like Champ," suggested Sandy, "you know, like Wamp, or Pamp, or something."

"Yer," said Zeb jeeringly, "or Tramp, and it would have legs and go marching round the place, or Damp, and you'd have to wipe your hands every time you touched it."

"Or Cramp," said Sandy, "and you'd get this awful pain every time you read it."

"Or Lamp," said Zeb, "and it would have a little light inside that went on when you opened it."

I could see they'd go on messing about for ever, and never get their minds back on the job, so I said sarcastically, "Why don't we just call it Stank, and spray a horrible smell all over it?"

They thought that was really funny, and so did I, actually, and we all rolled round laughing for a bit. Sandy stopped first.

"It's got to be funny," he said. "It's got to make them laugh. What about Laughs?"

"Or Smiley?" said Zeb.

We thought for a moment. Then we heard Dean and Jimmy and Lucy giggling like maniacs on the other side of the playground. A right load of gigglers they are.

"What about Giggles?" said Sandy.

"Bit girlish," I said.

"Rick's right," said Zeb. He was looking earnest and serious now. Zeb's got this thick black hair like a sort of doormat that sticks out over his face, and when he's thinking about something he pulls at it.

"Cackles then," said Sandy, listening to Dean, who laughs like a drain. He's nutty, really, Dean is. Loony. Daft. Potty.

And then it came to me, the perfect name, just like that, out of thin air, in yet another wonderful burst of genius.

"Crackers," I said.

There was a sort of silence, then Sandy did a rugger tackle on me, and Zeb sat on my chest, and they both kept on saying, "Brilliant, good old Ricky, what a genius, that's it, Crackers," so loud they didn't hear me screaming at them to get off.

But at that moment Mrs Kemp the dinner lady rang the bell, and probably saved my life.

Chapter Six

"Don't gobble your food like that," said Mum that evening, as I was having my supper. "It's not nice."

"He's got worms, I expect," said Dave, being horrible as usual. "They live down in your intestines and grow about a mile long, and eat all your food, and you get thinner and thinner and hungrier and hungrier." Just because Dave's thirteen, he thinks he knows everything.

"That's enough," said Dad. He doesn't hold with being disgusting at mealtimes.

"Yes, quite enough," said Polly, all prim and proper and irritating as usual.

"Sorry," I said, even though it was Dave, not me. I didn't want to start a row, because I was desperate to slip off quickly after supper and see Uncle Godfrey. I had to get him on my side. If he wouldn't let us use his photocopier, Crackers would never get printed. I put on my best face.

"Can I pop round and see Uncle Godfrey after supper?" I asked Dad. I knew he'd let me, even if Mum said no.

"What for?" said Dad. He was in a good mood this evening. Mum had made shepherd's pie for supper, Dad's favourite. When he's enjoying his food he puts his head down and shovels it in as if it was a race or something. It's not fair. If Dave or I did that, Mum would tick us off, but just because it's Dad, he gets away with it.

"I've got some homework I want to ask him about," I said, thinking quickly.

"I'll help you with it," said Dave. He likes doing my homework. It makes him feel grand

and superior. He likes telling me how much cleverer than me he is.

"You can't," I said. "It's a project on communications. I've got to make a sketch of a photocopying machine."

It sounded a bit silly even to me, but it was true. Nearly true, anyway. Miss Prout's always making us do daft things, like watching an egg boil and describing what happens, or turning a stone over and making a list of everything underneath it. She'd said we had to draw a machine that helps people communicate. Everyone else thought they were brilliant to think of drawing their telephones, but I didn't see why a photocopier wouldn't do as well.

"Whatever next?" said Dad, but he was holding a huge forkful of mash in the air, and dying to get on and eat it, so he just said, "OK, you can go," and bunged it in, and then because he'd taken such a lot in one mouthful, some of it got stuck in his moustache on the way into his mouth and he had to wipe it off.

Mum was trickier.

"I don't want you to be late, and I don't like you wandering round the streets in the evening," she said, looking worried as she began to clear away.

"I won't be wandering, honestly Mum," I said. "Straight to Uncle Godfrey's and back. It's a promise." And before she could say anything else I was out of the kitchen and off down the road.

My Mum doesn't really approve of Uncle Godfrey. She thinks he's wasted himself. She says it's high time he got married and had some kids of his own, instead of living with Julie, and being bossed around by her four kids. She says he should be turning his mind to earning a proper living and getting on in the world. I don't know what she's on about. Uncle Godfrey seems quite happy to me. He doesn't seem to see much of Julie anyway. He keeps out of her way most of the time, down at the bottom of the garden, in his workshop, where he has all his machines.

"Wotcher, Rick," he said, when I pushed open the door. "Come to wish me a happy birthday?"

I felt awful. I hadn't got a card or anything.

"It's not your birthday, is it?" I said. "If it is, nobody told me."

Uncle Godfrey laughed. "No, of course not," he said. "Only teasing. Here, have a wine gum, that is if your Mum doesn't disapprove." Uncle Godfrey always says that kind of thing about Mum. I don't think he likes her any more than she likes him.

It wasn't easy explaining about Crackers to a grown-up. I had sort of imagined that Uncle Godfrey would be really keen and excited, like me. But now he was there, rolling himself one of his smelly old cigarettes, and waiting for me to say why I'd come to see him, I felt it was a bit of a cheek to ask him. In the end, he guessed it, as soon as I started talking.

"And I suppose you want me to print your precious comic for you?" he said.

"Well, er . . ." I couldn't think of anything to say.

"How many pages is it going to have?" he said.

"I don't know," I said, feeling silly.

"Well, say it's six," he said. "How many do you want to print?"

That was easier.

"Oh, hundreds and hundreds," I said. The dream had faded for a moment or two, but it was coming back now. "We're going to sell them at school for 10p a copy, and . . ."

"Hang on a minute." Uncle Godfrey was jotting something down on a piece of paper.

"Look Rick, me old lad, it's going to cost a bit just for the paper, you know, and then there's the copying on top of that. I'll have to charge –" he scratched his head "– about £5 for fifty comics. And I'm mad to do it for that. That's going to work out at 10p a copy, and that will eat up all your profits. You're not going to make any money. You'll have to sell them for more."

I looked down at his piece of paper. I was so disappointed, the numbers swam about on the page. It was much more money than I'd expected. If Uncle Godfrey wouldn't let us pay for it by working for him, we'd never get Crackers going.

"Uncle Godfrey," I said, feeling embarrassed but sort of hopeful at the same time, "if we, I mean Zeb and me and Sandy, came along and did some work for you here, once a week, do you think, I mean would you . . .?"

Uncle Godfrey laughed and slapped his good leg with one inky hand.

"You're a right one, you are," he said. "You'll be a press baron one day, swanking round in a Rolls with a two foot cigar. OK, Ricky, you win. You can come round here after school for an hour or two on Mondays. That's my easy day. And you can help me clean this pigsty up a bit. And in return I'll . . ."

"Yes?" I said, keeping quite still in case somehow the spell stopped working.

"I'll print fifty copies a month of your precious Crackers for nothing. But it had better be good, mind. I don't print any old rubbish on these premises. Only the best will do."

Chapter Seven

I didn't get to be really good friends with Zeb and Bella till we did Crackers together. Zeb only came to our school last year, and he couldn't speak any English then. He still speaks a bit foreign, but I've got used to it. Zeb draws a lot. He used to draw all the time. I suppose he couldn't think of anything else to do, because he couldn't talk and no-one could read his kind of writing.

With Bella it was different. We've been in the same class ever since we were babies. Well, four, anyway. I don't get on much with girls usually. They giggle, and whisper, and everything. And they never take any notice of me. But Bella's different. She's wicked on roller skates, and she plays the drums.

Anyway, at our first meeting, Zeb had done these great pictures. He'd drawn a whole lot of round balls, and then added bits on to give them characters. They were really funny, like Devball, which had horns and a tail, and Handball, which had lots of hands and no legs, and Teachaball, with a teacher's board hat thing, and Speedball, whizzing along on a couple of thin little legs.

Sandy held the paper out and looked at it. He was frowning. I thought he was going to go grand and bossy, being the editor, and I was thinking how I could bring him down a peg or two, because I really liked Zeb's ball people, but all Sandy said was, "Yeah, it's great. Where do you think? Front page? Middle page?" and that was one whole page of Crackers drawn already.

I was getting sort of nervous about showing them Glossop. It was different this time, somehow. So I said, "Come on then, Bella, where's the girls' page?"

Bella put on a stuck-up look, and did a couple of ballet steps. Sandy was pulling a face and I could read his mind just as if he had a massive thinks bubble over his head saying, 'Girls!'

"Who says I'm going to do any silly old girls' page?" said Bella. "I'm going to do the cover."

"Hey!" I said, getting all hot and bothered. "That's not fair! Crackers was my idea. I'm going to do the cover."

Bella looked at me for a moment, then she stuck her tongue out and made her eyes go all googly. She's really pretty, Bella is, with curly black hair, and big brown eyes like Mrs Angelbeck's spaniel, but when she makes faces she's the worst. Or the best. Whichever way you look at it. After a moment she put her face back to normal and laughed. I could see she'd just been winding me up.

"Twit!" she said. "You should have seen your face! I don't mean it about the cover. But I'm not going to do any soppy girls' page. No-one'll buy it for that. The girls'll read it all if it's any good, and they won't read it at all if it's not."

She did a sort of boum-di-di-boum drum routine on the brick wall while we just looked at each other. Then she reached up her sweater and pulled out a sheet of paper.

"How about this, then?" she said, all careless-ly, but I could see she wasn't feeling careless. "It's new. I've called them the Lollihops. Look – it's a load of lollipop people all hopping about trying not to get licked."

It was good. Very good. We could all see that at once. I felt suddenly nervous. It was now or never.

"Want to see my new Glossop pictures?" I said, feeling my hands go sweaty as I pulled them out of my folder.

I'd spent hours on them the night before, and I'd done this ace story about Glossop trying to catch a fly for his dinner and falling splat on his face in a puddle, and the fly coming and sitting on his head. And he's lying there looking up at it with his eyes crossed.

Bella said, "Fantastic!"

And Zeb said, "Cool."

But all Sandy said was, "Very nice."

I could see he thought something was wrong, so I said, "Don't you like it, then?"

"Something funny in the first picture," he said. We were looking at it so hard, we forgot there was anyone else in the playground. Anyway, you have to have eyes in the back of your head if you want to see what Stevie Funny-Face Portman's doing. He's such a sneak he could make himself as flat as a dinner-plate and slide under a door if he really wanted to. He's always listening and prying and snooping and spying, that's Stevie. And then he goes and tells Dudley Big Mouth Parker and before you know where you are, your private business is all over the playground.

So there we were, me and Zeb and Bella and Sandy, having our meeting in the corner of the playground just near the steps that go up to the kitchens, and there was Sandy saying, "I think you'd better do the mouth again," when out of the corner of my eye I suddenly saw the familiar flash of Stevie's red and orange striped sweater (I suppose his mum makes him wear it so she can see him coming) and I whizzed round the corner and got him by the leg just as he was trying to get away.

He did graze his arm, but there was no need to scream loudly enough for Mrs Kemp to hear. At least, I didn't think so. But Stevie's such a cry-baby. He bawls the place down when he even gets a teeny tiny bit of red felt-tip on his finger, because he thinks he's pricked himself.

I got all the blame of course. Mrs Kemp wouldn't take any notice when I said he'd been spying on us.

"You just be careful, Ricky Sturgis," she said. "I'm going to watch out for you, knocking over other children like that," and she put her arm round Stevie and took him off to the medical room. She put the sticking plaster in the wrong place though, on his leg instead of over his mouth, because when he came out again he went round saying, "I know what you're up to," though he didn't really, and "Think you're clever, don't you," till Sandy said he'd mince him up and feed him to his gerbils. But he only said it once because he didn't want Dudley Parker to hear.

Anyway, after that, we decided we needed our own office where we could talk in private, and it was Bella who found it.

There's a big wall running round our playground. It's old and crummy, and bricks fall out of it sometimes, and then some men come and patch it up. Last year they did a big job on it, and put new tarmac on the playground as well, with a hopscotch painted on it and everything. But when the men left, they didn't take all their stuff away and a pile of tarmac and bricks and things got left behind, and after a bit it turned into a nice solid pile. You can get behind it, and if you have a look-out on top, you can see right across the playground, and no-one can sneak up on you because it's in the corner with two huge walls behind it.

Last year we'd never have got that place, because everyone wanted it, but now there's a new climbing frame and this craze for a sort of French cricket with rules that Kirk and Peter made up, so no-one was interested in the old tarmac pile any more.

So Bella and I marched across the playground, with Sandy and Zeb following, and we got up on the pile. And Sandy thought he should say something because he's the editor, so he put his hands on his hips and said, "I hereby claim these – er – what are they, Rick?"

"I dunno," I said.

"Offices," said Zeb.

"No," said Sandy, "prom–, prem–"

"Premises," said Bella.

"Right," said Sandy. "I claim these premises for Crackers. May God bless her and all who sail in her."

"Hang on a minute," I said. "That's for a ship, isn't it? And keep your voice down. You don't want the whole school to know."

"Stop arguing," said Sandy, "and listen to your instructions. Our next meeting is tomorrow, in these premises, at first break, and you'll have to bring two more pages, because we're going to bring out the first issue two weeks from today."

Chapter Eight

You never saw anyone change like Sandy did when we were doing our first Crackers. He got really bossy. I started getting fed up with him pretty soon. I mean, Crackers was all my idea in the first place, and I was the one who said he could be editor.

So there I'd be, every night, putting on these fantastic yawns, and saying I was going to bed early, and then getting out my precious drawing paper from its secret place under the newspaper on the floor of my cupboard, and drawing sheet after sheet till I'd done something brilliant, listening out all the time in case Dave was creeping up to my bedroom door, ready to burst in and catch me doing something he didn't know about.

And then the next day, old Sandy would hold out my beautiful cartoon at arm's length, and look it up and down, picking his nose, and then he'd say, "Not bad, but do the first bit again. I can't accept it like that," or "Why don't you make William the Waiter go splat into the water at the end? I think that'd be funnier than just running over the bridge."

And I'd say, "You try drawing someone going splat into the water. It's really hard. Bet you couldn't do it."

And he'd say, "Oh, well then, if you *can't* . . ."

And I'd grab it back, feeling furious, and I'd have to take it home and do it all over again.

But what made me really mad was that he didn't do the same to Zeb and Bella. Bella's Lollihops were great, but Zeb's Victor Vulture looked really knock-kneed, and its beak seemed to be coming off even, but Sandy just said, "Brilliant, magic, fantastic, well done."

After a week, though, we were nearly ready. We'd got Victor, and a page of Zeb's Sillyballs, and the Lollihops, and William the Waiter and a fantastic page of Glossop. Even Sandy agreed it was good enough for the front page.

Then, on the inside page, Glossop's hopping along all happy and cheerful, saying, "Hello, folks, I'm off to buy my copy of Crackers," and he doesn't realize it but he keeps making other

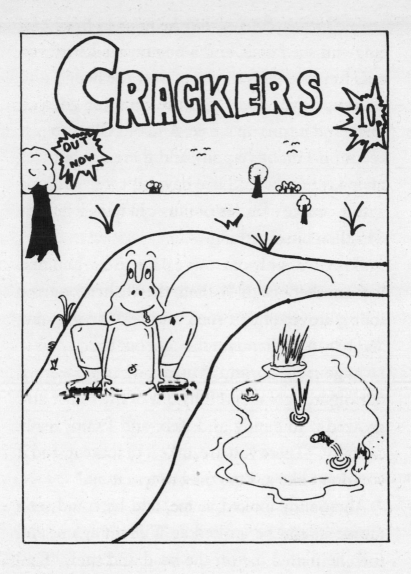

people have accidents, like he hops in front of a lady and she faints, and a boy on a bike tries to miss him and goes shooting over the hedge, and he jumps over a cat and the cat's fur goes all spiky and it runs up a tree. And old Glossop just keeps on smiling happily and there are bubbles saying things like, "Nice day, isn't it?" and one with a couple of notes of music in it, as if he was whistling or something.

There was only one more page to do, and that was another one of William the Waiter, pouring soup all over one of the customers by mistake, and I did it brilliantly. I thought out exactly what I was going to do, and at break, when we were in our office, I got it carefully out of my folder and showed it to Sandy and Zeb, and I said, really casually, "There you are, take it or leave it, and if you don't like it, I'm going to tear it up."

And Sandy looked at me, and he could see I meant it, and he looked at William again, and then he patted me on the head and said, "Brilliant, magic, fantastic, well done," and I put it back in its folder and patted him on his head, and on his back and his arms too, and he started patting me, only the pats got harder and harder. And suddenly there was Mrs Kemp standing right over us, and she said, "Stop fighting at once, you boys, or I'll report you."

Trust her not to know the difference.

Chapter Nine

You know what, if my Uncle Godfrey had been alive in the Roman Empire, he'd have been a slave driver, with a hairy chest, and a great big whip, and millions of slaves, and only half his front teeth.

We went round to his place the next Monday night with our lovely first issue of Crackers all ready to be printed. Only Bella wasn't there. She plays in her band on Mondays. We were sort of looking forward to working for Uncle Godfrey. So it came as a bit of a shock.

The workshop looked worse than ever. Mum says my bedroom's the end, but she doesn't know what she's talking about. Even she would have agreed that it's just the beginning if she'd seen Uncle Godfrey's place.

"Right, you lads," said Uncle Godfrey. "I want you to start by picking up all the rubbish on the floor."

He waved his hand round rather grandly, as if the place was Buckingham Palace or something.

"You can put all the junk in those cardboard boxes. Then I want it all swept, and those shelves over there tidied up."

I didn't dare look at Zeb and Sandy. If they felt like I did, they felt awful. It looked as if it would take all night.

"See you later," said Uncle Godfrey, and he started limping over to the door.

"Aren't you going to help us?" said Sandy. He wasn't used to doing anything at home. His Mum does everything for him.

"What? With my bad leg?" said Uncle Godfrey. "Not likely," and off he went.

We were still standing there, sort of frozen, gaping at the mess, when he stuck his head round the door again.

"Don't you touch the machines or anything, and I mean *anything*, mind, or I'll skin you," and then he disappeared again.

Once we got started it wasn't too bad really. We got loads and loads of rubbish off the floor. The boxes were soon full, and we had to get in them to trample all the stuff down so we could pack more in. It was fun, that bit, only Sandy kept shoving Zeb and me out of the way. He'd got fed up with doing the clearing up.

"You know they do grapes like this, for wine," he said, "when they haven't got all the machines and that?"

"Ugh, with your dirty feet?" said Zeb. "Don't be disgusting."

"It's true, isn't it, Rick?" said Sandy. "And all the pips and the skin and everything squidges up between their toes."

I was right down on the floor, fishing a whole lot of dirty old fag ends out from under one of the tables.

"And they specially don't wash their feet for

weeks so the wine tastes all fruity," said Sandy.

"Oh, shut up," I said. I was trying to sweep the cigarette ends into the dustpan, but I kept knocking the broom into all the machines.

"And it all squelches up their legs and everything," said Sandy.

Zeb got into another carton and started trampling too.

"And it splashes on the girls' knickers," said Sandy.

They both started laughing so much I knew I'd never get them back on the job, so I picked up a bit of paper we'd missed off the floor, made a dart and chucked it at Sandy. I'm not very good at darts usually, so it must have been just luck or something, but it went *ping*! right on his nose.

And then Zeb made another. Paper aeroplanes are his best thing. He once shot one right across the playground and in through the staff room window. We all hid behind a tree, and we saw Miss Prout get up crossly and look out and then shut the window, but she never found out who did it.

Anyway, a second later, there were all these paper aeroplanes zinging round the workshop, because there was all this waste paper on the table, too good to miss, and I did an ace, right up on to a top shelf, and Sandy hit the light twice, and then all of a sudden I saw the door open, and I yelled,

"Stop!"

But it was too late, because Uncle Godfrey came in, and it was really unlucky because he caught one of Zeb's jet-propelled stingers right in the eye. Lucky he wears glasses, if you ask me.

I was scared stiff for a moment, that he'd blow up and not do Crackers after all, but he only bent down, clutching his bad leg in the way he does, and picked up the dart, and said, "Not a bad little dart. At least you had the sense to use waste paper."

And then he looked round, and he must have been quite pleased, because it looked a million times tidier, even if we hadn't started on the shelves.

So he said, "Come on then, pass over your masterpiece, I haven't got all night," and a minute later, Crackers was rolling off the press, and Uncle Godfrey was reading it and laughing, and Zeb was trying to sort the pages out, and I was practising with the stapler and getting all the staples stuck in my fingers.

I can tell you, I didn't sleep more than a wink or two that night. To start with, it was really exciting and scary smuggling my pile of Crackers home and up the stairs and into my room without nosy old Dave or Polly catching me, and then hiding them under my bed. And then I was suddenly scared it would all go wrong, and Miss Prout would confiscate them all, and Mr Crook would get Mum and Dad up to the school to tell them I'd been wasting school time, and Mum would look all sad and disappointed again, like she did after the parents' evening. I must have gone to sleep then, because when I woke up next morning I felt quite different. I just knew it was going to be brilliant, and we'd stun everyone, and they'd all queue up to buy it, and Stevie Portman and Dudley Parker and Leroy and Pete and all their gang would be as sick as parrots.

Chapter Ten

The first amazing thing that happened that day was that Sandy was on the doorstep of our house practically before dawn. Before I'd finished my breakfast, anyway. Or found my shoes. Or put my sweater on. Or fed the goldfish.

Mum got to the front door first.

"Oh, it's you," she said, not sounding very pleased. "Bright and early today, aren't you?" and then Sandy bounced after her straight into the kitchen looking so excited you'd probably have got an electric shock off him if you'd tried to touch him.

"What are you looking so pleased about?" said Dave.

Sandy's face split into a great big grin, and he opened his mouth to answer.

"His grandma's come to stay," I said quickly, "and she's given him a fantastic new leather football."

Sandy's mouth stayed open with surprise. He looked at me really hard. I was dead sure everyone would see and get suspicious.

"What's in that big bag?" said Polly. That girl's so nosy her nose'll drop off one day. Serve her right.

Sandy didn't try to say anything this time. He just went on looking at me.

"It's library day," I said. "He's got hundreds of library books to take back."

I could see Mum's mouth going all prissy. I knew she was about to say something like, "At least some of your friends know how to read a book."

But I'd stuffed the last bit of toast into my mouth, and was off up the stairs to get my things. I was tired of thinking up silly answers to all their silly questions. It was too early in the morning.

"Haven't you told them about Crackers then?" said Sandy, as we whizzed down Penny Hill.

"'Course not," I said.

"Why?" said Sandy. "My mum thinks it's brilliant."

"It's all right for you," I said bitterly. "You don't know what my lot are like. They go on and on about everything. Polly would say it was silly and laugh, and Mum would say it was a pity I didn't put so much work into my schoolwork. Dad would be OK, but Dave would say he could do cartoons a million times better, and why couldn't he do one of his stupid caterpillars for it, and then he'd try to get all the money off me."

"Oh," said Sandy, but I could see he didn't understand. He's always going on about how lucky I am, having brothers and sisters. Some people don't know when they're well off.

The second amazing thing that happened that day was that we forgot to buy the Champ. *And* it was a Tuesday. *And* there was going to be a great new cartoon series they'd announced the week before. It just shows, doesn't it?

The third amazing thing was Miss Prout. As soon as we got to school, we started walking round with our piles of Crackers in our arms, shouting, "Roll up, roll up and buy Crackers!" (only Sandy was trying to be funny, shouting things like "Roll over," and "Roll on, roll off," and then he started singing that one that goes, 'So we all rolled over and one fell out, Hit the deck with a scream and a shout',) and everyone, even the little first year kids were fishing around in their pockets trying to find 10p, when Miss Prout came marching up and said, "What have you got there, Richard?"

So I said, "Crackers, Miss, it's our brand new comic."

So she said, "Let's see."

So I said, "It's 10p, Miss."

So she laughed and got out her 10p, and gave it to me, so I gave her a copy, and she looked through it and said, "Did you do all this yourselves?"

So I said, "Yes, me and Sandy and Bella and Zeb."

So she said, "Remarkable. Quite remarkable. Well done."

And off she went, and I could actually hear her cackling to herself as she went round the corner, her nose buried in William the Waiter. Imagine that. A teacher, spending 10p on our comic. And laughing. She must be human after all.

Chapter Eleven

It wasn't quite as easy selling Crackers as I thought it would be. I mean, people didn't just come up, and hand over their money and pick one up like they do in a shop. They kept saying things like, "Go on, Rick, let's have one."

So I'd say, "10p, please."

And they'd say, "But I gave you a packet of crisps last week," or "I haven't got it today. I'll pay you back tomorrow, honest."

Or even worse, they'd pull out a whole lot of pennies from their pockets, all stuck together with a disgusting old lollipop, and they'd say, "There's only 8p there, but I'll give you a couple of football stickers to make it up to 10p."

Zeb and I were the best at selling. We were really tough.

"No 10p, no Crackers," Zeb kept saying, and I was the same.

Bella was absolutely the best though. She got this tap dance routine going, and she yelled out, "Smicker smackers, nicker nackers, fetch your money and buy your Crackers!"

But Sandy was awful. He let about eight copies go for nothing but promises and a few bits of bubble gum.

Still, by the end of lunchbreak we'd sold millions. Forty, anyway. A whole load of girls had bought them, except for Clare and her friends, who spend all their time hanging round watching Dudley Parker, just because he's the biggest in the school, and going ooh-ah, all lovey-dovey and stuff like that.

And lots of people said they'd buy one tomorrow, only they hadn't got any money with them today, so I reckoned we'd sell the lot by the end of the week.

We had a meeting in our office at last break.

"Yah! yah! We did it! We did it!" yelled Sandy, dancing up and down. And Zeb did a cartwheel. He's really good at tricks like that. It wasn't a brilliant idea, though, doing a cartwheel, because all the money fell out of his pockets and rolled round all over the place. You wouldn't believe how far one little 2p piece could go. We had to run halfway across the playground for some of them.

When we'd got all Zeb's money back (all we could find, anyway) we did a count-up.

"I got £1.60," said Sandy.

"I got two quid," said Bella.

"I got more than you," said Zeb proudly. "Look," and he held out £2.20.

"Yes, but I got all this too," said Sandy, and he put down on the ground a horrible collection of old stickers, sweets, foreign stamps, a Superman pencil, a bouncy ball and a packet of coloured rubber bands.

"It's a load of rubbish," I said.

And Zeb said, "Yes, rubbish."

And Sandy said, "No it isn't, it's worth pounds and pounds, this lot."

So I said, "Well, who's going to pay pounds and pounds for all that stuff?"

"I am, and I'll bring the money tomorrow," said Sandy.

I knew he could afford it easily, because he gets so much pocket money, so I said, "OK then."

Altogether, with the £1.80 I'd made, we had £7.60. It wasn't exactly enough to make us millionaires, but it was a great start. And the sight of all those coins, real, and hard, and heavy, was better than all the dreams I'd had, even if it wasn't as much.

"I'm going to buy a colour TV with my share," said Sandy. He was still dreaming, obviously. Trust him to have big ideas.

"I'm going to get a new cassette," said Bella. She's like that, Bella. Realistic. She doesn't get all carried away.

"Hang on a minute," I said. "We're not spending any of this lot, not yet, anyway."

They all turned on me.

"What do you mean?" said Sandy. He looked like a little kid whose Mum's just taken the dummy out of its mouth.

I could see it would be tricky, trying to explain, but I knew I was right. I'd got this kind of feeling, deep down, that we needed to keep the money for emergencies. For a while, anyway.

"It's going into a special fund," I said. "We'll share it out later, when we see how things are going. We might need it for . . ."

"For what?" said Sandy.

But I never got the chance to answer because Zeb suddenly said, "Hey, look out,"

We looked round, and there was Dudley and Stevie and Leroy and Pete, all coming towards us in a line across the playground, looking really threatening and dangerous, and I just had time to scoop up all the money and get it into my pocket, then dodge off after the others. The rest of the day we spent trying to keep out of their way, and it was hardest of all for me, because the weight of all the coins in my trouser pocket almost made me lean over to the right whenever I walked.

Chapter Twelve

There was no doubt about it. Crackers was a brilliant, knock-out, champion success. Gold medal. Five star. World cup. But there were still a couple of problems.

The first one was that I didn't know where to keep the money. My Mum's got this sort of instinct about hiding places. She goes straight to them. She's like a human metal detector, only she's an everything detector.

Still, I must admit, I've made a few mistakes, hiding things. Once, when I was a little kid, I had this ice-cream and I tried to hide it so I could come back and finish it later, and I put it underneath my teddy on my pillow. *And* it was a hot day in the middle of summer. *And* it was a choc-ice. Mum had to change my whole bed.

And another time, when I was about three or something, I found this dead bird, and I sort of knew Mum wouldn't want me to play with it, so I hid it in my toy truck, and put it at the back of the toy cupboard, and forgot about it. And then we went on holiday for a couple of weeks.

You never saw anything like the state my Mum was in when she opened the front door and the stink came out at her. Polly went all green, and Dave wouldn't stay inside, but said he was going to sleep in the garden, and Dad looked furious and searched the house, and he found my poor old bird and buried it at the bottom of the garden. And then he spanked me.

Of course, I'm much better at hiding things now, but Mum's always poking about as if she didn't trust me or something. As if I'd still go about hiding dead birds. I mean, I was only three.

My best hiding place is in the bathroom.

There's a sort of hole in the bit of wood nailed round the bath where the pipes go in, and I can get my hand in there and hide things. It's a great place. And no-one can come in and surprise me because I can lock the door and pretend I'm doing something else. If you see what I mean.

So I sneaked a plastic bag out of the drawer in the kitchen, and put all the Crackers money in it, and stuffed it behind the bath.

"What have you been up to today?" Mum said at suppertime. She's always asking questions like that. She says things like, "What does Miss Prout say about your spelling, I'd like to know," or "Don't tell me you're still in the bottom group for language."

As usual I tried not to answer, but this time, Dad chipped in.

"Didn't you hear your mum, Rick?" he said, raising his head just long enough from his spaghetti to get his question out.

So I said, "Same as usual," and then I asked Dave to pass the salt.

"Don't take too much," said Mum. "It's not good for you. Hardens the arteries."

"Why does Dad have so much then?" I said, and that started her off as I knew it would, and she spent the next five minutes saying how Dad was asking for a heart attack, and she washed her hands of it. Dad gave me a filthy look, but at least I'd got Mum off asking questions.

And Crackers was still my secret.

Chapter Thirteen

The next problem was Dudley's gang. We knew they weren't going to like it, Crackers being so brilliant I mean. But we hadn't sort of thought about what they'd do.

They were all there, next day, when Sandy and I got to the school gate. Stevie started them off.

"Yer, think you're clever, don't you?" he said, swinging backwards and forwards on the gate like he's been told 90 million times not to. We took no notice.

"Think you're the most brilliant people in the whole world," he said, deliberately swinging the gate shut just as we tried to get through.

"That Crackers is a load of rubbish, anyway," said Leroy, but not too loudly. He only goes round with Dudley's gang because he's scared they'll pick on him if he doesn't. He's scared of everyone, Leroy is.

"Yeah, it's really stupid, a load of stinking old rubbish," said Pete. He's awful, Pete. At least, he's quite nice on his own, but he's awful when he's with Dudley.

Funny thing was, though, that Dudley himself didn't say a word. He just stood there, looking all dangerous and big, and letting all the others say everything.

I could feel Sandy beside me go stiff, like Tom in Tom and Jerry when he sees the bulldog. He's such a twit, Sandy is. He loses his temper and goes crazy, then everyone laughs at him, and he gets even madder and bashes someone. Then he gets into trouble for it. So I watched out for the moment when Stevie had swung the gate open, and I yelled out, "Look out, here comes Mr Crook!"

When they were all looking round (only Mr Crook wasn't there at all, of course) I grabbed Sandy and we got through the gate and raced into the school just as the bell rang.

There wasn't much Dudley's lot could do in school time, apart from Pete sticking his foot out and tripping me up when I went to get a pencil. But at break they were at it again. This time Zeb was with us too.

"Think you can draw, don't you?" It was Pete who started this time.

We didn't say anything.

"I can draw twice as well as you can, Rick Sturgis."

"No, you can't."

"Yes, I can. Three times as well."

"Don't be a big twit."

"Leroy's robots are just as good as Zeb's silly old Sillyballs anyway."

"No, they're not."

"Yes, they are."

"You couldn't draw Victor Vulture to save

your life, not even if you were hanging upside down over the biggest cliff in the world with Billy the Kid pointing a gun at your head."

"Yes, I could. Anyone could."

"No, they couldn't."

"Victor Vulture's dead easy."

"Prove it then."

"Why should I? It's silly, anyway."

"It isn't."

"'Tis."

"'Tisn't."

"'Tis."

They might have gone on for ever, but then Zeb did something really funny. He lifted his arms and hooked them round like wings, and frowned and pushed his lips out, and started flapping about, and he looked just like Victor. Lots of kids came round and laughed, and some of them said, "Got any more Crackers, Zeb, because I brought my 10p today."

No-one took any notice of Dudley and his gang. And they all went off chanting things like,

"Silly old Glossop, silly old Victor," but you could see they were just bluffing.

We sold another sixteen copies of Crackers that day, and I had £1.60 to stuff behind the bath. But on the way home, I saw Stevie and Dudley, heads together, talking really hard, and I knew they were up to something.

Chapter Fourteen

It was two weeks before we found out what Stevie and Dud had been plotting, and it was a nasty shock when it came. Sandy and I had met Zeb halfway down Penny Hill, and we were busy trying to decide what should go into the next Crackers.

"Not another Victor," said Sandy, being his bossy editor self again. "You'll have to do something new, like a joke page, or something. You know, those kind of spelling jokes like the one that goes 'How do you get rid of varnish?' 'You take the *r* out.'"

"What?" said Zeb. "What are you talking about?"

"Varnish, vanish," said Sandy, sighing. "Get it?"

"Yes, well, why can't you make Bella do something new then," said Zeb, who wasn't interested in jokes and always had to have them explained to him. "She said she's going to do the Lollihops again."

"Yes, but there's a story to the Lollihops," said Sandy. "It's a real . . ." and then he stopped talking and let out a noise, sort of like "Eek!"

Out today! ¬
New! Magic!
. Wot larfs!
Only 10p ,
Smashing /
free gifts

"Look at *that*!" he said.

We jerked to a stop. I don't know if our hair all stood on end, but if a cartoonist had drawn us it would have.

There, pinned on a tree, just outside the gate, was a notice, really badly written. I recognized the writing. It was done by Leroy Jones. He's in Dudley Parker's gang.

And there was Stevie, grinning from ear to ear, with a pile of paper in his arms, shouting out, "Roll up, roll up, and buy Wot Larfs! Much better than all the other comics! New jokes, cartoon strips and fabulous free gifts!"

He gave a sort of pretend jump of surprise when he saw us, though I bet he'd been watching out for us to come down Penny Hill.

"Oh, hello you lot," he said, all casual. "Aren't you going to buy Wot Larfs? It's the greatest! It's fantastic! And you get a lovely free gift too. Look, a sugar cigarette with each copy, not like some other mingy old . . ." then he saw Sandy's face, going white, then red, then practically purple, and he shut up, and started sidling away towards Dudley, who was selling another pile of comics on the other side of the gate. But he went on grinning like mad, and watching us.

"I'm afraid we're too busy to waste our time on that kind of thing, and anyway, sugar rots your teeth," I said and we swept past him, me on one side of Sandy, and Zeb on the other so he couldn't do anything violent.

At breaktime we had an urgent meeting in our office. Bella'd got hold of Karen Tucker, a little girl in the first year who's soft on Sandy, and we sent her off to buy Wot Larfs for us.

"It's terrible!" said Sandy. "Listen to this. 'Knock knock! Who's there? Eileen. Eileen who? I leaned over the garden wall.' That's the oldest joke in the world. It's prehistoric. I fell off my potty laughing at that one."

"And look at this," said Zeb. He pointed to a page of silly squares with faces and arms and legs.

"Sillysquares," he read out. "It's a rip-off! It's a cheat! They've copied us! It's not fair!"

"Let's have a look," I said, and I turned the page.

"Terry the teacher," I read, and there was this awful cartoon story about a teacher, really stupid and hopeless. Nothing clever and funny, like William the Waiter.

"It's so bad," I said, feeling better now I'd had a good look at it, "that no-one's ever going to buy it. They'll all stay loyal to Crackers."

"No, they won't," said Sandy, dancing about with rage.

"Why not?" I said. "Crackers is heaps and heaps better."

"Yes, but look," he said, and pointed. I saw what he meant. Kids all over the playground were laughing about with sugar cigarettes in their mouths, pretending to smoke, all grand and grown-up.

I heard Bella suck in her breath.

"Mandy Cootes!" she sort of hissed. "And

Sasha! And Emma!" And she zoomed off across the playground like a black-haired bullet.

"How did Dud's lot get all those free gifts?" said Zeb. "Must have cost a fortune."

"Stevie, of course," yelled Sandy. "His dad's got a shop!"

It was the last straw. It was so unfair. I felt this huge rush of rage, and I started punching and kicking into the air. Only the wall got in the way, and I punched it by mistake, and bashed my fist. The pain sort of took away the anger.

Sandy looked amazed. He's not used to me going bonkers. I'm usually the one who's stopping him smashing the place up when he loses his temper.

"What are we going to do, then?" said Sandy, quite quietly. Seeing me go off my head had calmed him down.

"Don't worry," I said. "We're not beaten yet. We're going to do another Crackers, and it's going to be so brilliant, and funny, and cool, and fantastic, and full of jokes, and stunning cartoons that their silly old Larfs will look like a load of babyish scribbles. Which is all it is, anyway."

Chapter Fifteen

After that, of course, it was war. Only instead of guns and bombs and submarines and everything, we were fighting with jokes and cartoon strips. Everybody knew Crackers was miles and miles better than Wot Larfs. And not only the first ones either. Crackers Number Two was a hundred miles better even than Crackers Number One. And Wot Larfs Number Two was even more stupid than Wot Larfs Number One. Sandy said it should have been called Wot Cries, and even old Zeb got that joke. But Wot Larfs kept on selling and selling, just because Stevie kept on giving out these stupid free gifts. With Wot Larfs Number Two you could choose be-

tween those pink rubbers that smell of straw-
berries and notebooks with pictures of Donald
Duck on them. They were good, even though
most of the covers were a bit torn.

"Stevie's dad's off-loading substandard
stock," said Zeb, frowning.

"Eh?" said Sandy.

"He's getting rid of stuff," said Zeb, "because
he can't sell it. They all do that. My uncle told
me."

Zeb's uncle works in a shop down the high
street selling TVs and radios, so Zeb knows all
about off-loading, and substandard and things
like that.

"Can't your uncle give us some free TVs and
hi fis to give away with Crackers then?" said
Sandy.

Zeb didn't even bother to answer.

"We'll just have to keep going," I said. I was
worried, I can tell you. The second Crackers had
only sold twenty-seven copies. It was bad luck it
came out on the same day as Wot Larfs Number

Two. At least, it might have been just bad luck, but I thought maybe Sandy had been talking too much as usual, and he'd boasted to Mandy or Clare or someone about when the new Crackers was coming out, and Dudley Parker's spies had probably found out and Dud had got Wot Larfs out on the same day deliberately.

The crazy thing was, though, that Wot Larfs was so awful nobody even bothered to read it. They just chucked it away when they'd got their free gift. But they all passed Crackers round the playground and really loved it. You could see two or three kids all trying to grab it off each other, and begging to borrow it.

It was very hard work getting Crackers Number Three ready. I was running out of ideas. I mean, it's all very well thinking up a new cartoon character, and doing lots of drawings of it, but when you've got to think up stories as well, it's difficult.

Glossop was OK. I had lots of ideas for him. In Crackers Number Two I had him squelching

around in this boggy place, and then a duck
comes along and tries to nibble him, and Glossop kicks out his back legs, and lands one on the
duck's beak, and it does a somersault, and goes
splat into a whole lot of icky mud. It was
brilliant. And in Crackers Number Three I
thought I'd call it Daddy Glossop, and Glossop
has millions of tadpoles and he gets a friendly
trout to babysit for him, and the trout's going
mad trying to stop them all swimming away
while Glossop's lying on the bank sunbathing.

The trouble was, I couldn't think up anything for William the Waiter.

"Make him spill some ice-cream down a customer," said Zeb.

"Idiot, he's spilled the soup already," said Sandy. "I know, why don't you make him give something disgusting to someone to eat by mistake, like a dead rat, or a load of spiders, or something."

"How do you think I'm going to draw a dead rat and a load of spiders?" I said. I mean, I know I'm brilliant, but there are limits.

"Yaroo!" shrieked Sandy, doing one of his victory yells right in my earhole and making me jump out of my skin. "I've got it! You could do that joke, you know."

"What joke?"

"The one about the waiter."

"What waiter?"

"The waiter in the restaurant."

"What restaurant?"

"Well, there's this man, right?"

"Yes."

"And he's been to the market, right, and bought a load of vegetables."

"Get on with it!"

"I am getting on with it!"

"So what happens next?"

"Right. So this man goes into the restaurant, and the waiter says, 'What would you like, sir,' and he says 'I'll have a steak and kidney pudding,' and the waiter says 'What about the vegetables,' and the man says, 'Oh, they can just have a sandwich.'"

So that's what I did. I drew Sandy's joke up into a cartoon. And maybe it wasn't all that

brilliantly fantastic, and I don't want to sound as if I'm boasting, but it was nearly as good as the Champ, even Sandy said so, and it was a million times better than Wot Larfs, that's for sure.

Chapter Sixteen

I don't care what Mum says about my uncle. He can be really nice sometimes. For instance, he could see I was feeling bad when I took Crackers Number Three round to get it photocopied.

"What's the matter with you?" he said. "You look like a dying duck in a thunderstorm. And what's happened to your mates? Fallen under a bus?"

"Don't think so," I said. "Sandy's mum says he's got to stay in because he's looking tired, and Bella's Mum's cross about her going out all the time, and Zeb might come along later."

"Getting bored with hard work, are they?" said Uncle Godfrey, heaving himself off his chair and limping over to the big photocopying machine in the middle of the workshop.

"No, it's not that," I said quickly, but I was beginning to think Uncle Godfrey was right. Zeb had said his dad didn't like him going out in the evenings, and Sandy had been really funny after school.

"See you at Uncle Godfrey's then, around half-six," I'd said, when he left me at our house, and he'd looked a bit sort of shifty, and then he'd said, "Sorry, I can't tonight Rick, honest. Mum says I've got to stay in. Says I've been doing too much and I've got to go to bed early."

But later on I'd heard him tell Lenny about Fizzlewick, that's on TV on a Wednesday night, and it's Sandy's favourite programme, and he was saying how he's never missed it once since it started, so I guessed maybe he just wanted to stay at home and watch it.

Uncle Godfrey was still looking at me.

"What's the problem, Rick, me old son?" he said.

So I said, "It's nothing."

"Stop messing about," he said.

"You wouldn't understand," I said.

So he said, "Suit yourself," and I told him all about it. I told him about Wot Larfs, and all the free gifts, and how awful the jokes were, and how the cartoons were all just copied from the Champ, and how mean Dudley and Steve and all that lot were. And I'd been right not to tell him straight away, because he just stood there and roared with laughter.

"Oh, my Lord!" he kept saying, "A circulation war in the playground! Whatever next!" And then he was off again.

"It's not funny," I said, and honestly, I felt like crying. "They've pinched our idea, and it's not fair, and . . ."

He must have seen I was upset because he stopped laughing, and he put his fists up and did a couple of pretend punches at me like he always does when he's being friendly.

"Cheer up," he said. "I'm not laughing at you.

If you want to know, I think you're a real Boy Wonder. Now, stop worrying. It's not the end of the world. You've just got to beat them and their Wot Larfs at their own game, see?"

"How can we?" I was suddenly furious. "We haven't got dads with shops with a whole lot of substandard goods to off-load."

"Oh, ho," said Uncle Godfrey. "You *have* learned a thing or two, haven't you?"

He seemed ready to burst out laughing again, but then he stopped himself.

"There's other ways to sell comics," he said. "You don't have to have free gifts."

"You mean, making it so good everyone will want to buy it?" I said bitterly. "We've tried that. It doesn't work. They all just borrow it from each other."

"No, no," said Uncle Godfrey. "I mean, look how they sell newspapers. They have tasty bits of scandal, and crossword puzzles with prizes, and competitions . . ."

"Competitions!"

Uncle Godfrey's jaw dropped open. I must have looked an idiot because I was hopping up and down like a madman.

"A competition!" I shouted again. "It's brilliant! And they'll all have to buy Crackers because they'll have to cut out a form and fill it in to enter for it. We'll have a competition for . . . for . . ." I was thinking madly. "For the best new cartoon character."

"And what about the prize?" said Uncle Godfrey.

"Never mind that," I said grandly. "We've got the Crackers fund, haven't we? We can buy something fantastic out of that. Here, Uncle Godfrey, don't worry about printing tonight, we've got work to do," and I grabbed the papers back from him before he'd even started the machine up, and streaked out through the door.

I heard Uncle Godfrey bellow after me, "Mind you all come next time. This place needs a proper tidy-up again."

Chapter Seventeen

You'd have thought that Sandy and Zeb would have been dead impressed with Uncle Godfrey's great competition idea. I told them about it in our Crackers office the next day, but they just stared at me, all glassy-eyed.

"Big deal," said Sandy.

"So what else is noo?" said Zeb. He watches too many American crime shows, if you ask me.

Only Bella was interested. She popped the bubble in her bubble gum, got it all back in a lump in her cheek and did a handstand.

"Good idea," she said, upside down. "But the prizes'll have to be brilliant."

Just then Dudley Parker came swaggering up,

and Stevie darted out from behind him and waved a stupid page of Wot Larfs right in front of our noses, and said in a horrible ner-nicky-ner-ner voice, "No-one buys silly old Crackers any more. Why should they, it's such a load of rubbish. So why don't you lot go and jump in the river?"

"And you can fall under a bus," said Sandy, going red as usual.

"And you can get lost in the woods," said Pete.

"And you can flush yourselves down the toilet," said Zeb.

Everyone looked at him, amazed. Zeb never usually says anything when there's a row going on. Not things like that, anyway.

"Think you're so clever, don't you?" shouted Sandy, really furious by now. "But you just wait and see. We're going to beat your silly old comic right out of this school. We're going to have a . . ."

But just before he said it, I grabbed his head

and stuck it under my arm, and put my hand over his mouth, and Zeb got his arms, and twisted them round behind his back so he couldn't get free, and I said in his ear, "Shut up, you great big twit, or you'll give the game away."

Still, there was one good thing about Sandy being such an idiot. After he'd said all that, we had to have a competition. We had to show them we meant business.

It was easy enough working out the rules. All we had to do was draw up a little box like this:

Competition!!!
Invent your own cartoon caracter!
Fabulus prizes
All entries to S. Baker before fri July 8

The really difficult bit was the prizes.

"We'll have to have three," said Zeb, "gold, silver and bronze like in the Olympics."

"Yes, but how are we going to pay for them?" said Sandy. "It'll cost a fortune to get really good ones."

"We'll get the money out of the Crackers fund, of course," I said. "I told you we had to keep it for emergencies. If this isn't one, an emergency I mean, I don't know what is."

"Yes, but I thought we were going to split the money between us," said Sandy, looking disappointed. He could see his colour TV disappearing out of the window. Not that he had a hope of buying one with about £3.10 anyway.

"Look, you idiot," I said. "If you sell loads of Crackers because of the competition, you'll get back the cost of the prizes and probably make still more money, so it's worth it."

"Yes, but what are the prizes going to be?" said Bella. "I mean, no-one's going to do the competition if they don't even know what the prizes are."

By the end of break we hadn't got anywhere near sorting it all out. Or by the end of school either. And I was still thinking about it at suppertime. I suppose I must have been in a bit of a daze because I didn't hear what they were all gassing on about, until suddenly I heard Dave say "Champ annual."

"What?" I said, coming to with a jerk.

"Say 'pardon'," said Mum, "and don't speak with your mouth full."

Dave was grinning at me.

"There's this bloke at school," he said, "and he's got these old Champ annuals, three of them, and he's selling them for a quid."

"What, each?" I said, hearing my voice go all squeaky.

"No, dope. A quid for the lot," said Dave, and if I'd been thinking about it, I suppose I'd have noticed a cunning look on his face.

"I'll have them," I said.

"You haven't got a quid," said Dave.

"That's all you know about it then," I said. "Been saving my pocket money."

"First I've heard of it," said Dave. "OK then, I'll phone him up and get them for you. Wouldn't mind looking through them myself, actually."

I saw it all then. Dave wanted to get the annuals for himself, but he felt a fool buying kids' books, and anyway, he didn't want to spend his own money. So he'd laid a trap for me, and once I'd bought them he'd take them all into his room and treat them like his own. Only Dave didn't know it; he wasn't going to get the chance. Those Champ annuals were going to be handed out as prizes, and at a quid the lot it was the bargain of the century.

Chapter Eighteen

It was Dave's turn to do the washing-up after supper, so that meant I could slip off without them all seeing me and go upstairs into the bathroom. But after that I was dead unlucky. The hole my money was in was a really tricky place to get at. You had to crawl under the basin and hook your hand in under the pipes. And it was just bad luck that I caught hold of the wrong end of the plastic bag, and half the money spilled out.

I went cold all over, listening to it rolling round under the bath. I got out the plastic bag with the rest of the money in it, and managed to reach quite a lot of the coins, but then I had to get right down on the floor with my nose pressed up against the drainpipe, to reach in for the rest. I reckoned there was only about 25p left in there, but I didn't want to lose it, after all.

I was so busy, fishing about under the bath, I didn't hear steps coming up the stairs. But suddenly the door handle rattled, and it was Polly.

"You can't *still* be in there, Rick? What on earth are you doing?"

"What do you think I'm doing?" I said, my head still under the basin.

"Your voice sounds all funny," she said, and I could hear her bump against the door as she bent down to look through the keyhole. Nosy! She's disgusting! Fancy looking at someone in the bathroom through the keyhole! Quick as a flash, I got off the floor and over to the basin, so she'd think I was washing my hands.

"Go away!" I yelled. "It's not fair, looking in like that."

It's a good thing Mum came up the stairs just then, before Polly had time to see everything. I heard her land a good wallop on Polly's behind, and then Polly went, "Oww!"

And Mum said, "Serves you right, miss, for peeping through keyholes," but then Mum started rattling at the door herself.

"Come on out, Rick," she said. "We all want to go."

So I said, "OK, just give me a tick to do my hands," and I flushed the toilet and turned the tap on so it would sound real, and quickly stuffed all the money I'd found back into the bag, except for £1 for Dave, and popped it back into the hole again. Only this time, I didn't push it right in, in case the money all spilled out next time I came to take it out.

And that's where I made my big mistake. I must have left a bit of the bag showing, because the next day, when I got home from school and was having a quiet biscuit in the kitchen, Mum put the iron down, and fished my bag of money out of her special drawer, and said, all casual like, "Know anything about this, Rick?"

I felt dreadful. Trapped.

"What do you mean?" I said.

"Because if you don't," said Mum, "I'll have to get Dad to get the truth out of you. So I'd own up, if I was you."

"It's mine," I said, feeling scared. I hate being found out more than anything else in the whole wide world.

"Where did you get it from, Rick?" Mum's voice didn't sound angry. It was quiet and reasonable, so I knew she was really serious. I didn't answer.

"You haven't been stealing, have you?"

That made me wild.

"Of course I haven't!" I shouted. "What d'you take me for?"

"All right, calm down," said Mum. "Where did you get all that money from? There's pounds and pounds in there."

There was no way out. I had to tell. I felt my tum go all wobbly. I was so sure she'd be furious about Crackers. I was so afraid she'd start on at me again, about wasting time, and not working hard enough, and not being clever, like Dave and Polly.

"I earned it," I said.

She looked even more serious.

"What have you been doing? Who's been paying you? What for?"

"It's the profits, from Crackers," I said, feeling like one of those spies in films who get tortured and have the truth pulled out of them bit by bit.

"What's Crackers?" said Mum.

So then I had to tell her everything, about Sandy and Zeb and Bella and Uncle Gregory and Dudley and Stevie and Wot Larfs, and she stood there, listening, as if she couldn't believe her ears.

"Do you mean to say," she said, when I'd finished, "that Godfrey's been making you clean up his filthy workshop for him, just for photocopying a few of your drawings?"

"It wasn't a few drawings, Mum," I said. "It was whole comics, loads of them, and they do look lovely."

But Mum wasn't listening any more.

"I'm going to give Godfrey a piece of my mind," she said, and marched off to the phone.

By suppertime, she'd calmed down, thank goodness. And then I had to show Crackers to the whole family. And the funny thing was, that when they were all sitting there, reading it, and turning the pages, and laughing at all the jokes, I was really glad it wasn't a secret any more. I felt good about it. Dad kept on laughing, and saying, "Fancy you doing all this and none of us knowing anything about it."

And Mum said, "Did you really think all this up yourself, Rick?" And then she looked at Glossop, and put her head on one side, and said, "It's really very good." And she gave me a new kind of look, sort of pleased and hopeful, as if maybe I wasn't such a fathead after all.

Dave was so impressed he didn't say much at all, for once. Even Polly was OK.

"Did you really do this William the Waiter?" she said, being her nicest self. "It's great. You'll be a famous artist, I expect, when you grow up."

"Oh, shut up," I said, trying to look all modest, but I didn't mind really. Actually, I liked it. My family don't usually tell me I'm clever. They usually tell me to get lost.

Chapter Nineteen

Everything about Crackers Number Four was great. For one thing, Uncle Godfrey didn't make us do a stroke of work.

"Got torn off a shred by your mum," he said, "for using child labour."

"You didn't use child labour," I said. "We volunteered. And anyway, you paid us. You printed Crackers for us, didn't you? And I've got the next issue here, with the competition and all."

"OK," said Uncle Godfrey, "but it's the last time, mind. I'm getting rid of this old photo-copier. Costs too much to maintain. I'm setting up a photographic business. Less messy."

"Oh," I said, but I wasn't surprised. Uncle Godfrey's always into something new. He ran a betting shop once, and then he had a wedding car business with a couple of fabulous old white Rolls Royces.

"Come on, then," he said. "Hand it over. Let's get on with it," and Crackers had whizzed off the machine and I must have been out of the door with it in under ten seconds. Well, ten minutes, anyway.

The next great thing was that Crackers Number Four was a sell-out. Well, I knew it would be. The four of us, Sandy, Zeb, Bella and me, had flashed those Champ annuals round the playground till everyone was dying to get one. We printed 70 copies of Crackers and they'd all gone by the third day.

It was a good thing they sold out so quickly, because Mr Crook came up to us when we were flogging off the last few and said, "I'm sorry, you lot, but I'm afraid I shall have to put a stop to this. It's illegal to sell things in the playground.

I've turned a blind eye to it so far, but there seem to be more and more of these comics coming out these days. You don't want me to get into trouble, do you?"

"No, Mr Crook," I said, but I didn't mean it. Mr Crook didn't mind getting me into trouble that time I climbed up on to the roof of the school kitchen, so why should I worry about him?

"But you can sell it outside the gate after school," he said, as if he was being really kind, and then he went back in to sharpen the chalks or count the dinner money or whatever it is he does in break.

I'd thought the competition was a good idea, but even I was surprised by how many of the school entered for it. Kids kept on coming up to Sandy, and shoving tatty bits of paper into his hands, and saying things like, "It's Larry the Lion, look, can't you see, there are his whiskers, and that's the tail, and . . ." or "It's Bimbo the Pirate. His hat's the best bit, don't you think?"

"How on earth are we going to judge this lot?" said Sandy, on Friday after school. "I mean, I'd like to give old Karen Tucker a prize because she's been really nice, and she desperately wants one."

"That's not how you run a competition," I said. Honestly, Sandy's hopeless sometimes. "You've got to be fair. Strict."

"Yes, but if you know it's by Dudley or someone, then you can't sort of look at it straight," said Sandy.

"We'll have to get someone outside to judge then," I said. "Someone who doesn't know anyone at school."

"Dave," said Sandy. "He likes cartoons. Do you think he'd do it?"

"What? My brother?" I said. "Have you gone off your head or something?"

"No, he'd be good, really," said Sandy. "He doesn't know any of the kids except us, and he found the prizes for us, didn't he?"

In the end, I said I'd ask Dave, mostly because

I couldn't think of anyone else. But I was glad I did because old Dave was great. He sat there for hours, very serious, and made three piles of good, bad and awful, then he split up the good pile into brilliant, super brilliant and world class. Then he picked out three and said, "There you are, gold, silver and bronze."

So I looked at the names on the back, and nearly fell over.

First prize went to Mandy Cootes for her Barmy Bats. Second prize went to Sam Dalyell for his Solomon Seal, and third prize went to Leroy Jones, number three in Dudley Parker's gang, deadly enemy of all of us, for his Puffballs.

"You can't give a prize to Leroy," I said to Dave. "He's in Dudley's gang."

"Fair's fair," said Dave. "Those are the best."

"But I'll look such a twit, giving Leroy a Champ annual," I said.

"That's your problem," said Dave. "I've judged them for you, like you said, and those are the best three. Take it or leave it."

So I had to take it.

Chapter Twenty

It's funny how you can get the wrong idea about people. I mean, I'd always thought Leroy Jones was just an awful little pest, hanging round Dudley and spying for him and everything. But he was so pleased about getting a prize in the competition, I changed my mind about him.

He kept bobbing about all morning, saying, "Did you really like mine third best? I mean, you know, I never thought you'd like it, because Glossop's so good. I mean, I thought you'd just chuck it out or something because I go round with Dudley. First time I've ever won anything in my whole life anyway."

And then he looked a bit worried and said,

"Do you think Dud'll get me, because it was a Crackers competition?"

And I said, "Not if you say he can borrow your Champ annual whenever he wants to."

Honestly, I have to do everyone else's thinking for them more than half the time.

We had a Crackers meeting in our office the day after we gave out the prizes.

"What next then?" said Sandy. "I suppose we could do another competition or something."

No one said anything.

"I don't feel like doing the Lollihops any more," said Bella. "I've got bored with them, somehow."

I knew what she meant. I'd gone off Glossop too.

"Anyway, it's the end of term next week," said Sandy. "We can't do anything in the holidays." He sounded pleased about it.

"Next term then, I suppose," said Zeb.

"But it's September next term, and football starts," said Sandy. "We won't have time."

"And then we'll all be doing the Christmas play," said Bella.

"And Uncle Godfrey's given up his photocopier," I said.

"That's it, then," said Sandy. "That's the end of Crackers. You'd better hand the money round, Rick."

I felt really sad. But it was no good. I could see it was the end.

"OK then," I said. "I'll bring it tomorrow. It'll be about a fiver each."

"Brilliant," said Zeb.

"Not bad, really," said Bella.

"Suppose not," said Sandy.

"I'm going to go down the High Street tomorrow and spend mine," said Bella.

"Me too," said Sandy.

"So am I," said Zeb. "I'm going to buy a new football shirt. What about you, Rick?"

But I didn't bother to answer him. I'd had an idea. A fabulous, gold-plated, diamond studded, smash-hit idea.

"Listen," I said. "You know what we're going to do? We're going to bring out a sports' magazine next term, and it's going to have interviews with the school's star football player, and . . ."

"Idiot, that's Dudley," said Sandy.

"So what?" I said. "And there'll be quizzes on the Olympics, and . . ."

"Who's going to print it?" said Sandy.

"My Mum will," said Bella, dancing about, pretending to whack a tennis ball over a net. "They've got a new photocopier where she works. She told me."

"See?" I said. "And there'll be tips from Mr Banister on improving your play, and . . ."

"I'll be the editor," said Sandy.

"And there'll be badges for people who buy it regularly, and . . ."

"Yaroo!" shouted Zeb.

"And you know what?"

"No, what?" said the others.

"It's going to be the greatest! Number one! Top of the charts! World class!"

Also by Elizabeth Laird

ON THE RUN

A daring rescue plan to save the life of a brave young soldier.

It's the civil war – and Hania has made an amazing discovery: a wounded Freedom Party fighter in the foothills near her grandfather's farm.

She tries to nurse him back to health in secret – but her grandfather finds out!

Will he betray Hania's soldier?

"a meaty read but its direct language will appeal to any adventure-loving child aged between 8 and 11."
BBC Family Life

Robert Swindells

THE SIEGE OF FRIMLY PRIM

The children of Frimly Prim hear their school is to be closed down and decide there's only one thing they can do; sixteen of the top class decide to occupy the school.

It's fun but it gets tricky until one very old lady and one little girl with a teddy bear come to rescue.

"A splendidly funny story . . ." *Books for Keeps*

By the winner of the Carnegie Medal.

Michael Morpurgo

THE SANDMAN AND THE TURTLES

To a city boy, summer holidays on the Welsh coast are
paradise. Mike always has fun with his cousins, and he
could listen to his grandfather's stories for hours,
although he thinks Polly is silly to believe the stories are
true.

But this summer it's different; Dadci's stories really do
come alive in a very special and wonderful way. Mike and
Polly have their best holiday ever when they encounter
the Sandman and the turtles.